Creeptastic

The diary of a
misunderstood creeper
and how he saved Steve's life.
(An *unofficial* Minecraft
autobiography)

**By,
Dr. Block**

*Hey, guys, if you like this book, **please leave a review**
where you bought it so other Minecrafters can learn
about it. Thank you!*

Table of Contents

Chapter 1

My first memory is of darkness. And then, slowly, the world got brighter, or maybe my eyes were just adjusting to the moonlight.

I looked around for a while, trying to see something. The first thing I saw was an ugly green and black thing. When I turned my head, the ugly thing was gone. But then I looked back, and I saw it again.

I soon realized that I was looking into a dark pool of water, and I was looking at my own reflection. And, boy, was I ugly! I was mostly green with gray and white spots here and there. My eyes and mouth were as black as pitch.

It made me very sad to realize that I was so hideous, but I must have been spawned for a reason other than to bring ugliness to the world. I needed to discover what that reason was.

But, how would I find out what my purpose in life was? I had no idea. I decided to start wandering around to see if I could find anything or anyone who could help me.

I walked for a long time in a flat, featureless landscape. I was bored and lonely.

Eventually, I made it to a forest with oak and birch trees. I bumped into an oak tree, and it did not feel good. I hissed at the tree, but the tree did not do anything. I guess my purpose in life was not to hiss at trees.

A few minutes later, I saw eight red eyes glowing inside a nearby cave. I walked over to the cave and saw that the glowing red eyes belonged to a small, young spider with a bluish tint.

I hissed at the cave spider. He hissed back.

I had found my first friend. I was very happy.

"Why do you live in this cave?" I asked the spider.

"Because, I hide from a mysterious figure. If he walks by, I try to jump on him from behind and bite him and kill him."

I was frightened by the spider's evil and vicious desire to kill. "Why do you want to kill the mysterious figure?" I asked.

The spider hissed again. "Because he kills other spiders with his iron sword."

"Maybe it is self-defense," I suggested.

The spider hissed at me and said, "You are stupid and ugly. Go away."

And that is how I lost my first friend.

I was very sad that I was alone again, but the cave spider

was mean and I did not like him anymore.

Chapter 2

About an hour after I left the spider's cave, I noticed the world becoming brighter. I had never seen so much light.

As it became brighter, I noticed a glowing square rising in the east. Somehow I knew it was the sun. I was born in darkness. Would I be able to survive in so much light?

But, before I could worry about the light for too long, I saw something so terrifying, I am almost unable to write about it.

I saw a burning zombie. I rushed over to him and tried to push him into a pool of water to put out the flames, but he moaned at me and pushed me away.

"I have to get to the village," he said in a grumbling voice.

"Why?" I asked.

"To eat the villagers," he said with a deep and emotionless voice.

"That is horrible. Why would you want to do that?" I asked.

"Because I am a zombie, you ugly green creeper noob," he said.

"A creeper? I am a creeper?" I said.

The burning zombie stopped walking and looked at me like I was a fool. "Duh, noob. Of course you are a creep–."

But before he could finish, the zombie burst into flames and died, leaving only a small pile of rotten flesh. Gross.

I later learned that zombies die from light exposure and this zombie died because he was talking to me because I was a noob and didn't know anything. I was responsible for this poor creature's death. I felt as sick as my green skin looked.

But, at least I now knew what I was: a creeper. But, I still did not know what my purpose in life was or *why* I felt like I needed to find something or someone to make my life complete.

I decided to go to the village to see if I could talk to anyone there. Maybe they could help me with my quest.

Chapter 3

When I got to the village, I tried to talk to a priest, a blacksmith, and a librarian. But they could not understand my hissing, and I could not understand the strange noises coming from their squishy mouths.

I could tell when the villagers looked at me, they only saw my ugly exterior. They were repulsed and frightened. Even if we could have understood each other, I knew they would not have helped me.

I was about to leave the village when I saw ... him.

I felt drawn to him. I felt like I could not live without being near him. But, I did not know *why* I felt this way.

All I knew was that he was **Steve**.

Don't ask me how I knew his name. It was as if the knowledge was hardwired into my brain when I was spawned, and it just took seeing him for me to remember him.

Steve was trading with a farmer to try and get some emeralds. I noticed the emeralds were green, like me. But, the emeralds were beautiful and I was ugly. Why didn't I shine like a beautiful emerald?

I started to walk toward Steve, like I was being drawn to him by some invisible force. Even if I had wanted to go somewhere else, I could not have resisted the pull of Steve.

Steve looked over at me and I could tell that he was afraid of me. Why? Why would he be afraid of me? I may have been hideously ugly, but I was full of love for Steve.

Steve stuffed his newly-acquired emeralds in his pockets, and started to run away. He could run very fast.

I followed him. I needed to get to him for some reason I still could not understand.

Unfortunately, he was too fast and was soon out of sight. But, I still felt his pull and knew that I would walk for the rest of my life just to get close to him.

"One day, oh Great One," I hissed aloud. "I will get close to you."

Chapter 4

As I left the village, I walked in the direction Steve had gone. I walked as fast as I could, but my four stubby little green legs did not go very fast.

"Curse you, stubby legs," I hissed and wailed aloud.

I was so sad. I had discovered that my purpose in life was to be near Steve, but I still did not know *why* that was my purpose. It did not make any sense. I did not even know Steve, so why would I need to be close to him?

And, even though I would never harm him, Steve ran away from me when he looked at me. It must have been because I was so ugly.

Why was I cursed with this horrible green, blocky body? Why?!?!?

I walked alone for hours. I passed trees and rocks and pools of water and lava, but saw no other creatures.

Suddenly, I heard a rustling sound coming from the bushes next to me. I turned to look at it. Who or what could be in the bushes? Maybe I could meet a new friend? I was so lonely.

But it was not a friend.

Out from the bushes came the most hideous creature I have ever seen. It was even uglier and more terrifying than me. It was a brown spotted creature about two feet tall, with four legs and a long tail. It meowed at me.

I felt true, bone-chilling terror for the first time in my life. It was the opposite of the joy

I felt when I first saw Steve. I was terrified to my ugly green core. I turned and ran from the ocelot as quickly as I could.

I could hear the ocelot chasing me. It was much faster than me. It jumped on my blocky green head and sank its claws deep into my green flesh.

"Ahhhhh," I hissed with pain. If I had arms, I could have pushed it off, but I did not. I was helpless against its terrifying attack.

The ocelot meowed and laughed at me. "What are you,

foolish creeper, some kind of noob?"

"What do you mean, you hideous beast?" I screamed.

"Don't you know you should stay away from ocelots? That we are the enemies of creepers?" the ocelot said as he let go of my head and jumped to the ground.

"No, I only spawned yesterday. I don't know anything," I cried. I was wishing I had arms to check the scratches on my head.

"That is why you are a noob," said the ocelot, laughing at me as he walked away back to his bush.

Chapter 5

"Why was everyone always calling me a noob?" I hissed aloud as I wandered away from the ocelot's bush. "I spawned last night. I can't learn everything in one day."

I stopped walking and stood still, trying to pick up the location of Steve. I felt a faint sensation that told me the direction to go to find Steve. I started walking towards him.

After I had walked for a few more hours, it was getting dark again. I was not scared of the dark. In fact, I liked the dark because I had been born in the dark and no one could see my ugly green body except other creatures of the night.

When it was pitch black, I heard two creatures yelling at each other nearby.

"No, you are the stupid one."

"I'm not stupid. You are the one who shot yourself with an arrow yesterday."

"I only shot myself because I was trying to shoot you and you were so scared you hid behind a rock and the arrow bounced off the rock and hit me."

"You still shot yourself, noob."

"Don't call me a noob! I spawned three days before you. If anyone is a noob, it's you."

I walked closer to these creatures to get a better look. Because I could see at night, I saw they were skeletons. What a strange world I was born into with zombies and skeletons. Who knows what else lived here?

I walked up to the two skeletons and hissed, "Hello."

They stopped fighting and looked at me. "What do you want, creeper?" said one of them.

"I want to find Steve."

The skeletons laughed. "The only thing you creepers ever want to do is find Steve. You guys are so boring."

"Guys? You mean there are more creepers than just me?" I couldn't believe it. I was not the only hideously ugly green blocky thing alive in the world.

"What are you, some kind of noob?" said one of the skeletons.

"Why does everyone keep calling me a noob?" I asked, hissing and whining at the same time (which is actually pretty hard to do).

"Because you are one. You don't know anything," said the other skeleton.

I was sad because I kept being insulted by everyone I met. I just wanted to learn how this world worked. Why didn't anyone help me? I decided I was not going to let these skeletons insult me. I had had enough!

"I may not know everything," I said. "But I do know one thing."

The skeletons laughed. "Yeah, right. What one thing is that?"

"I know that **Steve is love; Steve is life**," I said with conviction.

The skeletons started laughing so hard, I thought they might fall apart into piles of bones.

"See?" said one skeleton to the other. "He's a total noob. He doesn't even know what creepers are supposed to do to Steve." And they started laughing even harder.

"What do you mean? What am I supposed to *do* to Steve?" I asked. Finally, I would learn *why* I was drawn so strongly to Steve.

But before they could answer, they actually did fall apart into piles of bones, each with a single arrow on top. They had laughed themselves to pieces and died.

I stood over their piles of bones and shook my head sadly at how the meanness of the skeletons had caused their own demise.

"Who's the noob now?" I hissed.

Chapter 6

I left the skeleton bones and started walking east toward the horizon where the sun was beginning to rise. I sensed Steve was in that general direction.

I walked for hours until the sun was high in the sky. I walked past beautiful red poppies and lovely yellow dandelions. If only I had arms, I would have picked some flowers and smelled them.

I was sad again because the world seemed to be against me. No one liked me, and I was alone. The skeletons had said there were more creepers like me, but I had yet to see any. I thought maybe they were lying to me because they thought I was a noob.

But, then, I heard a familiar hissing sound. In fact, I heard lots of hissing sounds. It sounded like the hissing sound I made.

I forgot about Steve for a moment and walked as quickly as I could toward the hissing sounds. The noise seemed to be coming from the other side of a large blocky boulder.

I walked around the boulder and saw an amazing sight: ten creepers hissing to each other.

"Hi, guys," I hissed excitedly.

"Hi," they all hissed back.

"My name is ... uh ... well ... uh ... I ... uh ... guess I don't have a name," I said sadly.

"What are you, some sort of noob? Creepers don't have names," said one of them.

"We don't?" I asked.

"Of course not," said another.

"Why don't we have names?" I asked.

"I don't know," said a third one. "Creepers just gonna creep, man."

"Gonna creep? What does that mean?" I was so confused.

"We creep until we find Steve."

Suddenly, I became very happy. They were looking for Steve too. Maybe we could find Steve together.

"I saw Steve yesterday," I said excitedly.

They all looked at me with shocked expressions. Their black mouths hanging open. "Where? Where did you see him?" They all asked.

"In a village near the forest, about a day's walk from here."

"We must go there," one said.

"Why?" I asked. "Steve is no longer there. He went to the east, toward the rising sun."

"He did? How do you know?" asked one of the creepers.

"I sense him. I have been following the sensation. Don't you sense him too?" I asked.

"Not unless we are very close. It seems your Steve sensor is very powerful. You should lead us to Steve," one of them suggested.

The happiness inside of me was so powerful, I started to shake. I was shaking faster and faster. Suddenly, I felt very warm.

"Look out," screamed one of the other creepers. "He's going to explode."

My happiness left me and was replaced by an intense fear. I stopped shaking and became very cold. "What do you mean? Explode?"

"Seriously? You don't know?" they asked.

"I didn't know I could explode," I confessed.

"Yes, that is what creepers do. We find Steve and then we explode. But, sometimes we can explode if we get too excited."

"What do you mean, we find Steve and then explode? Why would we do that?" I asked.

"Because, a creeper's purpose in life is to kill Steve," hissed one of the creepers menacingly.

"No!" I screamed. "Steve is love. Steve is life."

"You are a fool," said another creeper. "Why would you think such nonsense?"

"When I saw Steve, I knew he was a great man. I knew that I would do anything for him. I knew that I would follow him forever."

The creepers looked at me like I was not only a noob, but a crazy noob.

"We are sorry you feel that way. But, thank you for telling us where to find Steve. We will

take care of him," said another
creeper.

"No," I hissed. "I can't let you
— ."

And then a large block of iron
ore landed on my head and
knocked me out.

Chapter 7

When I woke up, a wolf was licking my face. I wanted to pet the wolf to thank him for waking me up, but I did not have any arms. So, I just hissed, "Thank you, wolf." The wolf smiled at me and walked away.

I was alone again. But, I was not sad anymore. Instead, I was angry. I had to stop the gang of creeper assassins from killing Steve.

I stood up and felt dizzy. That block of iron ore did not feel very good. I could tell I had a big bump on my head. I could not believe my own kind would push a block of ore onto my head. The thought made me even more determined to stop them.

I looked down and saw the footprints of the creepers heading to the east. I started following them, walking as quickly as I could.

I soon realized that I would never catch up with the creeper assassins just by walking. I had to move more quickly. But how? I couldn't fly. I couldn't swim. I couldn't even run.

I kept walking and thinking about how to go faster.

After an hour, I had followed the tracks of the creeping pack of murderers up a mountain path, and they were still nowhere to be seen.

From my location, I looked down and saw a horse grazing on grass about twenty feet below me at the bottom of a sheer drop.

The horse was wearing bronze armor, so it must be tamed.

Horses are fast, I thought. What if I could ride a horse? I had no idea if my plan would work, but I had to try. I had to save Steve.

I walked to the very edge of the mountain and looked down. I lined myself up with the horse's back and then I jumped.

"Ahhhhh," I hissed as I fell through the air.

I landed on the horse with a thud and somehow managed to stay on his back. The horse bucked me a couple of times, and

I almost fell off. I was gripping the horse's back with my four stubby legs. I had to stay on. If I fell off, I'd never be able to get back on.

"Stop, horse, you have to help me save Steve," I hissed.

When the horse heard me say "Steve," he stopped trying to buck me off. He turned his head and looked at me.

"You are ugly," he said.

I sighed. "I know. I know. But, will you help me save Steve?"

"I know Steve," said the horse. "He tamed me."

"Why aren't you still with him then?" I asked, amazed and honored to be riding Steve's very own horse.

"We were attacked by a bunch of zombies and Steve told me to run away to save my life," said the horse. "I haven't seen him since then."

"Well, I have seen him, and he is in danger from a gang of creeper assassins. You must help me save him," I begged the horse.

"But, you are a creeper," said the horse. "Why would you want to save Steve?"

"Because," I said, "Steve is love. Steve is life."

"I believe you, creeper. I believe you because no creeper would ever say that unless he really meant it."

"Thank you, horse," I said. "I would stroke your mane, but I don't have any arms or hands."

"That is okay," said the horse. "I understand."

I looked to the sky and saw the sun was beginning to set. "We don't have much time," I said to the horse. "The creeper gang will catch up to Steve just after dark. He won't stand a chance. We must hurry."

The horse neighed and then galloped toward the east. We soon located the footprints left by the creepers, and the horse followed them as quickly as he could.

I hoped we would not be too late.

Chapter 8

About thirty minutes later, we heard an explosion coming from up ahead.

"Oh no," I said to the horse, "we might be too late."

The horse galloped as fast as he could. When we got close enough, we saw the creeper gang had pushed Steve up the side of a mountain. The creepers were following him up the mountain.

Steve was cornered. The mountain was so steep that Steve could not climb any higher. Soon, one of the creeper assassins was sure to get close enough to blow him up.

Steve was shooting at the creepers with a bow and arrow, but his position on the mountain was so precarious that he had a hard time lining up a good shot. He would not be able to kill them all.

I jumped off the horse and ran over to the creepers.

"Stop it," I hissed. "You have to let Steve live."

"Stand aside, noob," said one of the creepers. "Let the real creepers do what needs to be done."

The creepers walked past me like I wasn't even there. They were starting to form a pyramid, climbing on top of each other to get closer to Steve. It would not be much longer before Steve would be within their blast radius.

I started pacing back and forth. What could I do? How could I save Steve?

I stood at the edge of the mountain and looked down at a pool of lava below. Just then, I had a brilliant idea. If I could somehow push the creepers into the lava, I could kill them and save Steve.

But how?

I asked myself, what would Steve do?

And then, I knew what I had to do.

I had to sacrifice myself to save the great Steve from the creeper horde. Steve needed to live in order to build a bigger and better world out of block-shaped objects, one block at a time.

I walked toward Steve. I felt his power and love flowing through me. I felt so happy that I started to shake even though I was still very far away from Steve. I could feel myself becoming very warm.

One of the other creepers looked at me with horror. "What are you doing?" he hissed.

"I am saving Steve. He is love. He is life," I said.

"No," screamed the creeper. "You wouldn't dare."

But I did dare.

Chapter 9

Hi, guys, this is Steve writing now. I wanted to finish the story of the bravest, most honorable creeper I have ever known.

I watched as the creeper blew himself up in the center of the creeper horde. Some of them died instantly, while others were blown into the lava below and burned to death.

All of the dead creepers, except the brave one, dropped gunpowder. This creeper dropped a diary. By some magical process I don't yet understand, the diary had recorded all of this creeper's thoughts and acts.

You have been reading this same diary. I only wanted to write a few more words in it so you would understand that this amazing creeper's sacrifice was not in vain.

When I read this diary, I was humbled and inspired. To honor this creeper's sacrifice, I will continue to put even greater effort into my mining and crafting work in the Overworld and beyond.

And to any hostile mobs out there who might read this book, I say:

I am still alive.

I am still here.

This is *my* world.

The End

Thanks

Thank you so much for reading *Creeptastic*! Now that you are done, could you do me a favor and **leave a review** where you bought it? It is the equivalent of giving a high-five, and I love getting high-fives.

Thanks again.

More Books

Hi, guys! Do you want to know when the next unofficial Minecraft autobiography is coming out? Then go to **DrBlockBooks.com/join** to sign up for the Dr. Block newsletter.

If you liked this book, you will like my other books, including:

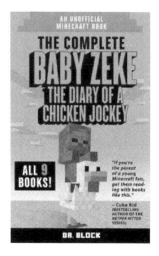

Made in the USA
San Bernardino, CA
27 June 2020